W9-CYB-316

NANCY DREW

girl detective
®

Writ In Stone

STEFAN PETRUCHA • Writer
SHO MURASE • Artist
with 3D CG elements by RACHEL ITO
Based on the series by
CAROLYN KEENE

New York

Visit us at www.abdopub.com

Library bound edition © 2006

Spotlight, a division of ABDO Publishing Company Inc., is the
school and library distributor of the Papercutz books.

Library of Congress Cataloging-In-Publication Data

The Haunted Dollhouse
STEFAN PETRUCHA – Writer
SHO MURASE – Artist
with 3D CG elements by RACHEL ITO
BRYAN SENKA – Letterer
CARLOS JOSE GUZMAN
SHO MURASE
Colorists
JIM SALICRUP
Editor-in-Chief

ISBN 10: 1-59707-008-4 paperback edition
ISBN 13: 978-1-59707-008-9 paperback edition
ISBN 10: 1-59707-009-2 hardcover edition
ISBN 13: 978-1-59707-009-6 hardcover edition
ISBN: 1-59961-059-0 library bound edition

All Spotlight books are reinforced library binding and manufactured in the United States of America.

Writ In Stone

NANCY DREW HERE. I'M THE ONE YOU BARELY SEE (OR CAN'T SEE YET), PANICKING AS THE LAMP'S ABOUT TO FALL.

BABYSITTING'S NOT MY USUAL GIG. USUALLY, I'M A DETECTIVE HERE IN RIVER HEIGHTS.

BUT OWEN ZUCKER'S MOM, ELLEN, HAD AN EMERGENCY AT ONE OF THE MANY FUNDRAISERS SHE WORKS FOR, AND SHE'S SUCH A SWEET WOMAN, I LIKE TO HELP WHEN I CAN.

OWEN WASN'T GENERALLY TROUBLE, BUT HE'D GOTTEN INTO THE COOKIES WHILE I WAS THINKING ABOUT AN OLD CASE, AND HAD JUST A BIT TOO MUCH *SUGAR* IN HIM!

WRIT IN STONE
CHAPTER ONE:
ROCKS AND ROLLS

THEN AGAIN, I COULD'VE BEEN *OUTSIDE* IN THIS MESS, INSTEAD OF SAFE, SNUG AND JUST A *LITTLE* ANNOYED.

LIKE THIS POOR TRUCK DRIVER, WHO WAS PROBABLY JUST *WISHING* HE'D STAYED HOME.

DRIVING A RIG THAT SIZE IS A TOUGH AND *DANGEROUS* JOB, ESPECIALLY IN THE RAIN.

THE WAY I UNDERSTAND IT, SOMETIMES WHEN YOU BRAKE, THE TRAILER WHEELS IN THE BACK *LOCKUP* SO THEY CAN'T SPIN.

IF THE FRONT'S STILL MOVING, THE REAR SWERVES SIDEWAYS INTO WHAT THEY CALL A *JACKKNIFE*.

I GUESS, BECAUSE IT MAKES THE TRUCK LOOK LIKE IT'S *FOLDING*, THE WAY A JACKKNIFE DOES.

IN ANY CASE, YOU DON'T WANT TO BE AROUND A TRUCK IF IT DOES THIS.

OWEN AND I HEARD THE CRASH A *MILE* AWAY. ABOUT HALF AN HOUR LATER, THE PHONE RANG.

WHAROOMMM

IT WAS CHARLIE ADAMS, TOW-TRUCK OWNER. HE'D PULLED ME OUT OF DITCHES A DOZEN TIMES AND NEEDED A FAVOR IN RETURN.

EVERYONE *OKAY*, CHARLIE?

THEY TOOK THE TRUCKER TO THE HOSPITAL, BUT HE WAS CONSCIOUS.

THIS GUY'S SUV'S TOTALED, BUT OTHER THAN HAVING ANTS IN HIS PANTS, HE SEEMS *OKAY*.

ANTS?

HE'S SO WORRIED ABOUT THIS CASE HE'S *CARRYING*, HE *REFUSED* TO GO IN THE AMBULANCE, AND WOULDN'T EVEN OPEN IT UP IN THE RAIN!

THIS IS THE CLOSEST *DRY* PLACE I COULD THINK OF.

THANKS FOR SAYING WE COULD DROP BY. I'M SURE MRS. ZUCKER WON'T MIND.

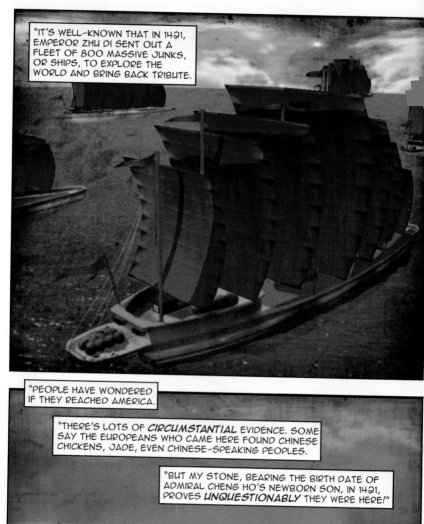

"IT'S WELL-KNOWN THAT IN 1421, EMPEROR ZHU DI SENT OUT A FLEET OF 800 MASSIVE JUNKS, OR SHIPS, TO EXPLORE THE WORLD AND BRING BACK TRIBUTE.

"PEOPLE HAVE WONDERED IF THEY REACHED AMERICA.

"THERE'S LOTS OF *CIRCUMSTANTIAL* EVIDENCE. SOME SAY THE EUROPEANS WHO CAME HERE FOUND CHINESE CHICKENS, JADE, EVEN CHINESE-SPEAKING PEOPLES.

"BUT MY STONE, BEARING THE BIRTH DATE OF ADMIRAL CHENG HO'S NEWBORN SON, IN 1421, PROVES *UNQUESTIONABLY* THEY WERE HERE!"

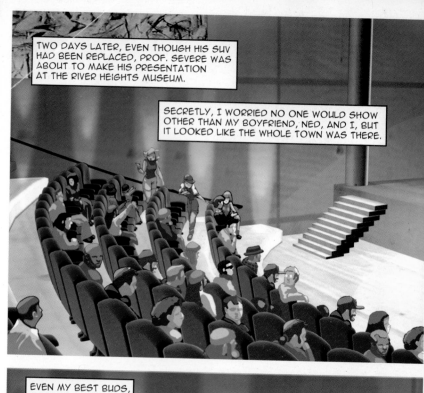

TWO DAYS LATER, EVEN THOUGH HIS SUV HAD BEEN REPLACED, PROF. SEVERE WAS ABOUT TO MAKE HIS PRESENTATION AT THE RIVER HEIGHTS MUSEUM.

SECRETLY, I WORRIED NO ONE WOULD SHOW OTHER THAN MY BOYFRIEND, NED, AND I, BUT IT LOOKED LIKE THE WHOLE TOWN WAS THERE.

EVEN MY BEST BUDS, GEORGE FAYNE AND BESS MARVIN.

YOU MADE IT!

I'M NOT BIG ON *HISTORY*, BUT IT WAS A GOOD CHANCE TO TEST OUT MY NEW HEAVY-DUTY POCKET VIDEO CAMCORDER!

HEAVY DUTY? I ONLY HAD TO FIX IT *TWICE* SO FAR!

BESIDES, WHO'D MISS A CHANCE TO SEE *YOU* DRESS UP! OH, NANCY, *PLEASE* LET ME PUT SOME EYELINER ON YOU!

EASY, GIRL! THE PRESENTATION'S STARTING!

THANK YOU ALL FOR COMING. USUALLY I ONLY SPEAK TO OTHER PROFESSORS, SO I'M NOT SURE WHERE TO BEGIN.

ANYONE HERE KNOW MUCH ABOUT CHINA'S *HISTORY*?

YES?

I'M *BORED*! WHEN DO WE SEE THE OLD ROCK AGAIN? MY MOM SAYS IT'S OLDER THAN SHE IS!

OWEN!

15

PRO-FESSOR, ANY IDEA WHAT HAPPENED?

NO.

DID YOU LEAVE THE CASE WITH ANYONE ELSE?

NO.

LEAVE IT ALONE AT *ALL*?

FOR A MINUTE IN THE WASHROOM BACKSTAGE AS I CLEANED UP FOR THE SHOW!

MR. BIRMSTROM, YOU'RE THE MUSEUM DIRECTOR! ANYONE ON YOUR STAFF HAVE ACCESS TO THE WASH-ROOM?

UM.... JUST THE *GUARD*, NANCY, NATE WENTLEY!

ANY REASON *HE'D* TAKE THE STONE?

I SHOULD HOPE NOT! YOU CAN SEE HIM YOURSELF, HE'S PROBABLY STILL IN THE BASEMENT.

17

HE'S A *GOOD* MAN, BUT WE DON'T PAY MUCH.

POOR FELLOW HAS TO HOLD DOWN *THREE JOBS* TO COVER HIS RENT, BUT THAT DOESN'T MAKE HIM A *THIEF!*

NO, BUT IT DID MAKE HIM A *SUSPECT.*

THE RIVER HEIGHTS MUSEUM HAS A *NICE* COLLECTION, BUT NOTHING AS *VALUABLE* AS THAT SHORE STONE MARKER!

THAT COULD PROVE *TEMPTING* FOR SOMEONE DOWN ON THEIR LUCK.

I HAD TO MOVE AS FAST AS I COULD, BEFORE THE TRAIL GOT COLD.

MR. WENTLEY! WAIT!

MR. WENTLEY!

AS HE PASSED UNDER A LIGHT, I COULD SEE HE WAS WEARING A HEARING AID.

WAS HE TRYING TO GET *AWAY*, OR JUST HARD OF *HEARING*?

THE DETECTIVE SIDE OF MY BRAIN WAS THINKING THE *WORST*.

THE PROBLEM WITH THAT DETECTIVE BRAIN IS THAT WHILE IT'S *GREAT* ON *CRIME* DETAILS...

MR. WENTLEY! PLEASE OPEN THE DOOR! I JUST WANT TO *TALK* TO YOU!

SLAM

...SOMETIMES IT DOESN'T PAY ATTENTION TO ANYTHING *ELSE* GOING ON.

LIKE WHERE I AM, OR HOW EASY IT MIGHT BE TO *TRAP* ME THERE!

IT TOOK JUST A FEW SECONDS FOR ME TO REALIZE I WAS LOCKED IN, BUT *TWO MINUTES* TO REMEMBER I HAD A CELL PHONE.

SLAM

BY THEN MR. WENTLEY WAS LONG GONE.

THANKS, NED!

SURE THING, BUT NEXT TIME WHEN YOU RUN OFF, COULD YOU AT LEAST SAY READY, SET, *GO*?

I HAD NO IDEA *WHERE* YOU RAN OFF TO!

AH, I LIKE TO KEEP MY BOYFRIENDS *GUESSING*.

BOY-FRIEND*S*? THOUGHT I WAS THE ONLY ONE!

YOU *KNOW* IT!

MY LIFE'S WORK...

DON'T WORRY, PROFESSOR, THE POLICE WILL BE HERE ANY MINUTE.

BETTER YET, NANCY'S PROBABLY *ALREADY* SOLVED THE CRIME.

NOT QUITE, GEORGE. PROFESSOR, ABOUT WHAT TIME WERE YOU IN THE WASHROOM?

ONLY A FEW MINUTES BEFORE I STARTED.

SAY, IS *THAT* THE WASH-ROOM?

YES, WHY?

GEORGE, *YOU* WERE IN THE SECOND ROW, BEHIND ME, RIGHT?

YOU KNOW IT. WHAT'S UP?

WELL, IF YOU WERE SHOOTING WITH YOUR NEW CAMCORDER, YOU HAD A *VIEW* OF THE WASH-ROOM!

SO THE TAPE MAY SHOW THE CROOK LEAVING! LET'S SEE!

YEAH, ONLY THAT THING'S SO *SMALL*, I SEEM TO HAVE *MISPLACED* IT!

HOURS LATER, WITH HALF THE TOWN LOOKING FOR HIM, OWEN WAS *STILL* NOWHERE TO BE SEEN. NEITHER WAS NATE WENTLEY OR GEORGE'S *CAMCORDER*.

SHH! ONE... TWO... THREE. *THREE* SQUIRRELS HIDE FROM *CAT!*

UH-OH! CAT GETS *CLOSER!*

HA-HA! CAT SAYS, "I *GOT* YOU!"

WHY DON'T YOU LET ME HAVE THE NICE *CAMERA*, THEN I'LL TAKE YOU *HOME*?

I'LL GIVE YOU SOME *CANDY*?

NO!

OW!

WORRIED AS I WAS ABOUT OWEN, I HAD A HUNCH HIS DISAPPEARANCE WAS CONNECTED TO THE STONE, AND MY ONLY CLUE THERE WAS NATE WENTLEY.

WHEN HE WASN'T AT HOME, I FIGURED THE BEST PLACE TO FIND HIM WOULD BE AT HIS SECOND JOB. AND YOU WOULDN'T *BELIEVE* WHERE HE WORKED AT NIGHT.

HE HAD A LIGHT STEP, BUT I COULD HEAR EARTH CRUNCH BENEATH HIS FEET, AND THE LIGHT FROM HIS LANTERN SWAYED AS HE MOVED.

SO I COULD KIND OF TELL *WHERE* HE WAS.

UNTIL THE SOUNDS JUST *STOPPED!*

AND I COULDN'T FIGURE OUT *WHY...*

UNTIL IT WAS TOO LATE!

AHHHH!

AHHHH!

I GUESS THE MOOD HAD GOTTEN TO ME AND GEORGE, TOO, BECAUSE WE DIDN'T BOTHER TRYING TO EXPLAIN OURSELVES, WE ALL JUST TOOK OFF!

IN FACT, WE WERE SO BUSY *RUNNING*, I BARELY NOTICED THAT OUR SUSPECT TOOK OFF IN THE *OTHER* DIRECTION!

OF COURSE, WHILE I WAS WATCHING *HIM*, I DIDN'T SEE WHERE I WAS GOING!

YIKES!

HER HEAD KNOCKED THAT CHUNK CLEAN *OFF* THE HEAD-STONE!

NANCY? NANCY?

GEORGE, I DON'T THINK SHE'S *BREATH-ING!*

OH MY GOD!

NANCY DREW IS *DEAD!*

END CHAPTER ONE

OF *COURSE*, OWEN IS MORE IMPORTANT! I'M JUST CONVINCED THE TWO MYSTERIES ARE *LINKED!*

BUT I CAN'T CONVINCE CHIEF McGINNIS!

I'M *SURE* YOU'LL FIGURE SOMETHING OUT, NANCY.

MEANWHILE, JACK HALLORAN AND I ARE SKIPPING OUR GOLF GAME TO JOIN THE SEARCH PARTIES.

THANK-YOU, HANNAH!

YOU KNOW, MR. DREW, MY COUSIN *JEDEDIAH* WAS *ALWAYS* RUNNING OFF WHEN HE WAS A BOY! SOMETIMES *HE'D* BE GONE FOR DAYS, TOO!

HIS MOTHER'S HAIR WAS *WHITE* BEFORE HE TURNED SEVEN!

REALLY? I WAS THINKING OWEN WAS *KIDNAPPED* BY THE THIEF, BUT MAYBE HE JUST RAN AWAY!

WHERE'D YOUR COUSIN *GO* WHEN HE RAN AWAY?

LIKE ALWAYS TRYING TO DO THE *RIGHT THING* NO MATTER WHAT IT TAKES! EYES ON THE PRIZE, LIKE DAD SAID.

SO IF THE POLICE WOULDN'T QUESTION NATE WENTLEY, I FIGURED I'D BETTER DO IT MYSELF!

IF HIS HOUSE *WASN'T* ABANDONED, IT *SHOULD* HAVE BEEN. GEORGE SAID WHAT WE WERE ALL THINKING...

LOOK AT THIS PLACE! AND HE HOLDS DOWN *THREE* JOBS! I ALMOST DON'T *BLAME* HIM FOR STEALING THE STONE!

LOTS OF PEOPLE FALL ON HARD TIMES, GEORGE. *FEW* RESORT TO STEALING! AND POSSIBLY *KID-NAPPING!*

WHAT YOU SAID, NANCY!

KNOCK KNOCK

KNOCK KNOCK

AHH!

I KNEW BESS WOULD BE *WORRIED*, BUT I FIGURED I HAD A DECENT CHANCE OF GETTING AWAY WITH IT, CONSIDERING MR. WENTLEY'S *HEARING* PROBLEM.

-CREAK-

OF COURSE, THAT DIDN'T MEAN I FELT COMFORTABLE MAKING *NOISE*!

FROM THE *OUTSIDE*, I COULD TELL THE HOUSE WASN'T IN GREAT SHAPE, BUT THAT DIDN'T PREPARE ME AT *ALL* FOR THE *KITCHEN*!

HANNAH WOULD HAVE A FIT! ME, I JUST FELT KIND OF SICK.

AND, OF COURSE, RIGHT ON TOP OF THE ROACH PILE, SAT A *PERFECT* CLUE – NATE WENTLEY'S *BANK STATEMENT*!

I WAS TRAPPED ONCE IN A GARDEN SHED FULL OF *SNAKES*, SO THIS WAS NO PROBLEM, REALLY...

WELL, *MOSTLY* NO PROBLEM.

BUT HERE WAS ANOTHER MISSING PIECE TO THE PUZZLE, A RECENT DEPOSIT FOR $10,000!

WHERE ELSE WOULD HE GET THAT TYPE OF MONEY, EXCEPT FOR *SELLING* THE STONE?!

I COULDN'T JUST *TAKE* IT, HE'D KNOW I WAS HERE. I ONLY *WISHED I* HAD GEORGE'S CELL PHONE CAMERA!

SPEAKING OF CELLS, MINE WAS VIBRATING.

IT WAS BESS. NO NEED TO ANSWER. I KNEW WHAT IT MEANT!

NATE WENTLEY WAS HEADING FOR THE KITCHEN – AND *ME!*

I WASN'T AFRAID HE'D *HURT* ME, BUT HE COULD HAVE ME *ARRESTED!*

BUT WHILE THE BANK STATEMENT WAS *IMPORTANT,* IT WASN'T PROOF! I NEEDED SOMETHING *MORE,* AND THIS COULD BE MY *BEST* CHANCE TO GET IT!

INSTEAD OF LEAVING, I DECIDED TO CHECK OUT THE *BASEMENT!*

JUST IN TIME, TOO! I COULD HEAR HIM RUMMAGING AROUND JUST THE OTHER SIDE OF THE DOOR.

I COULD ONLY HOPE HE'D DECIDED TO FINALLY *WASH* SOME OF THOSE DISHES!

THERE ARE A FEW THINGS EVERY GOOD DETECTIVE SHOULD ALWAYS CARRY, LIKE A *FLASHLIGHT*!

I ALWAYS MAKE SURE I HAVE MINE, EVEN WHEN I *FORGET* MY CAR KEYS!

THE PLACE WAS A MESS, THE SAME AS UPSTAIRS, BUT THEN I NOTICED SOME KIND OF *POWDER*.

IT WAS DIFFERENT FROM THE FLOOR, A LIGHTER *COLOR*, MORE LIKE SHORE MARKER!

COULD HE HAVE *DESTROYED* IT? WHY? MAYBE HE JUST *DROPPED* IT.

EITHER WAY, I NEEDED A *SAMPLE*. I DIDN'T HAVE A TEST TUBE, SO I MADE DO WITH THE TOP OF BESS'S EYELINER.

I ALSO DECIDED *NOT* TO MENTION IT TO HER UNTIL I COULD BUY A NEW ONE.

NOW, I HAD TO WORRY ABOUT GETTING *OUT*.

TELL GEORGE TO HONK THE HORN.

WHAT? WHY? ARE YOU *OKAY?* CAN YOU SPEAK UP?

BESS, I'M FINE. JUST TELL GEORGE TO HONK THE HORN!

HONK HONK

I WAS A LITTLE WORRIED THE HORN WOULDN'T BE LOUD ENOUGH, BUT IT *WAS!*

IF I COULD PROVE THE DUST WAS FROM THE SHORE STONE, HALF THE CASE WOULD BE SOLVED!

FORTUNATELY, WE STILL HAD A VISITOR IN RIVER HEIGHTS WHO WAS AN *EXPERT* ON THE MARKER!

47

THANKS FOR AGREEING TO TALK TO ME, PROF. SEVERE!

ARE YOU ALL RIGHT? YOU'RE *LIMPING*.

BAD KNEE ACTING UP, I'M AFRAID. HOW'S OUR GREAT DETECTIVE TODAY?

NOT SO *GREAT*, REALLY. SORRY I HAVEN'T BEEN ABLE TO FIND THE SHORE MARKER YET.

OH, IN THE END IT'S JUST A *ROCK*.

ANY WORD ON THE MISSING BOY?

NO. I THINK THE CROOK MAY BE HOLDING HIM BECAUSE THAT *CAM-CORDER* HAS A VIDEO OF THE CRIME!

I EVEN THINK I KNOW *WHO* IT IS!

OH? *WHO*?

WELL, *FIRST*, COULD YOU TELL ME, IS THERE ANY REASON SOMEONE WOULD WANT TO *DESTROY* THE MARKER?

DESTROY IT? I SUPPOSE.

I SPENT THE NEXT FEW HOURS WITH **NED**, SEARCHING FOR OWEN. BUT THE ONLY THING WE FOUND WAS THAT LONG WALKS IN THE WOODS CAN REALLY TIRE YOU OUT!

WHEW! MY LEGS ARE **KILLING** ME. IT'S LIKE TRYING TO FIND A NEEDLE IN A HAY-STACK!

WHAT ABOUT THE CASE OF THE MISSING STONE? YOU HAVEN'T SAID MUCH ABOUT IT!

BECAUSE IT'S DEAD-ENDED! I WISH I KNEW **SOMEONE** WHO COULD **REALLY** TEST THAT POWDER I FOUND.

HERE.

WHAT?

YOU'RE A **DREAM**, NED!

KEN BRADLEY, A PAL OF MINE FROM THE UNIVERSITY, IS **INTERNING** AT THE AMERICAN MINERALOGICAL SOCIETY. TELL HIM I SAID HI!

JUST DON'T SAY I NEVER GET YOU ANY-THING!

NED NICKERSON, EH? YOU *MUST* BE NANCY DREW! ANY GIRLFRIEND OF *HIS* IS A *FRIEND* OF MINE.

POWDERED STONE ARTIFACT, EH?

CAN'T TELL YOU HOW *OLD* IT IS, UNLESS THERE ARE MICRO-ORGANISMS, BUT I CAN TELL YOU *WHAT* IT IS, MAYBE FIND OUT IF IT'S THE TYPE OF *STONE* THE CHINESE USED.

I'VE HEARD SOMEONE MIGHT WANT TO DESTROY THE STONE BECAUSE OF WHAT IT MIGHT PROVE.

NED SAYS YOU HANG IN ACADEMIC CIRCLES. EVER MET ANYONE WHO MIGHT REALLY *DO* THAT?

NAH! NO ONE AT RIVER HEIGHTS UNIVERSITY!

IT'S PRETTY *OPEN* INTELLECTUALLY — WE'VE GOT ONE PROF WHO BELIEVES ALIENS BUILT THE PYRAMIDS!

OVER-NIGHT ME THAT SAMPLE. I'LL GET ON IT RIGHT AWAY!

WHEN I TOLD PROFESSOR SEVERE I'D BE SENDING THE SAMPLE OUT— HE SEEMED A LITTLE *FLUSTERED.*

I GUESS HE DOESN'T WANT TO DEAL WITH THE POSSIBILITY THAT THE STONE'S REALLY *GONE.*

IT'S KIND OF LIKE HIS *BABY,* I GUESS.

SPEAKING OF BABIES, I JUST CAN'T BELIEVE THE LITTLE GUY'S STILL *GONE!*

I KNOW IT'S CRAZY, BUT I FEEL LIKE IT'S *MY* FAULT SOMEHOW, LIKE I SHOULD HAVE FOUND HIM BY NOW.

I JUST WISH OWEN WERE HERE, *SAFE* WITH ME!

CAN'T MAKE OUT THE LICENSE! IT LOOKS LIKE IT DOESN'T *HAVE* ONE!

HELLO, *POLICE?*

YES, CHIEF McGINNIS, I THINK IT WAS ON *PURPOSE!*

OF *COURSE*, IT WAS ON *PUR-POSE!*

I'VE GOT A FEELING WHOEVER IT WAS JUST DIDN'T WANT ME TO DO...

...THIS!

OVERNIGHT MAIL

"IT LOOKS KIND OF *FAMILIAR*."

○rec 03:04:00

≈YAWN≈

I'M *BORED*. THIS ISN'T SO *FUN* ANY MORE.

-RUSTLE--RUSTLE-

UH-OH! BAD GUYS!!

HEE-
HEE!

QUITE A *SMART* LITTLE FELLOW, EH, OWEN? YOU COULD HIDE FROM *ANYONE!*

OH, I *KNOW* YOUR NAME NOW, IT'S ALL OVER TOWN.

WHAT HAVE YOU GOT, SOME HIDEAWAY UP THERE?

QUITE *REMARKABLE!* PROBABLY GOT A LITTLE BED OF *LEAVES* FOR YOURSELF UP THERE, TOO, JUDGING FROM YOUR CLOTHES!

END CHAPTER TWO

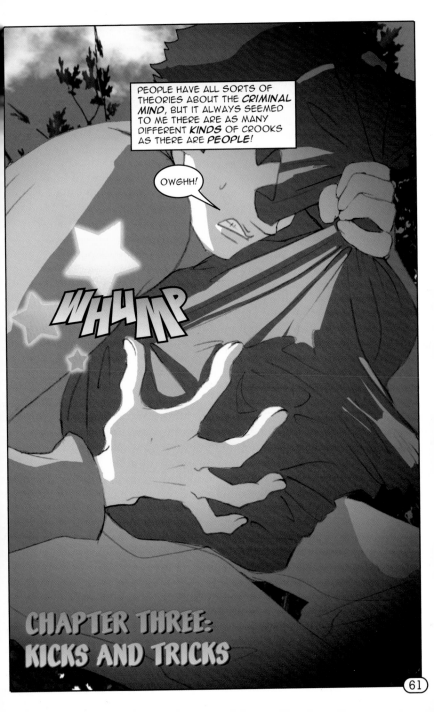

PEOPLE HAVE ALL SORTS OF THEORIES ABOUT THE *CRIMINAL MIND*, BUT IT ALWAYS SEEMED TO ME THERE ARE AS MANY DIFFERENT *KINDS* OF CROOKS AS THERE ARE *PEOPLE!*

OWGHH!

WHUMP

CHAPTER THREE:
KICKS AND TRICKS

67

OHMIGOD!

MRS. ZUCKER'S LITTLE DARLING *ERASED* EVERYTHING GEORGE TAPED AT THE PRESENTATION!

ANOTHER DEAD END! I'M SO SHOCKED, MY LEG'S *TINGLING*, LIKE IT'S GOING *NUMB*!

NANCE, THAT'S YOUR *CELL*. IT'S STILL SET TO *VIBRATE*.

OH, YEAH. THANKS!

KEN!

SO?

YOU FINISHED THE TESTING? UH-HUH. I UNDERSTAND. THANKS!

THE MYSTERY'S PRETTY MUCH *SOLVED*, BUT WE STILL HAVE TO CATCH THE CROOK!

AND I *THINK* I'VE GOT A PLAN! DOES OWEN HAVE SOME *CRAYONS* AROUND?

Y'KNOW, MY BEING A *VEGETARIAN* REALLY HONES MY INVESTIGATIVE INTUITION, AND I SMELL SOMETHING'S *UP!*

THERE ISN'T ANYTHING YOU'RE *NOT* TELLING ME, RIGHT?

MARLETTA, EVERYTHING I SAID IS *ABSOLUTELY* TRUE!

YEAH, BUT WHAT I SAID *WASN'T* ABSOLUTELY *EVERYTHING* THAT WAS TRUE. LIKE, I FAILED TO MENTION THE *REASON* WE DIDN'T HAVE THE TAPE WAS BECAUSE IT WAS *ERASED*.

SO, NANCY, WE'D BETTER GET GOING... TO THAT *PLACE*... TO DO THAT *THING*, RIGHT?

RIGHT!

ER.... A *PLACE* FOR EVERY *THING*, AND A THING FOR EVERY *PLACE*, I ALWAYS SAY.

OH, MY POOR CAMCORDER, I HARDLY KNEW YE!

SORRY, GEORGE. IT'S *GOT* TO LOOK *REAL*.

THUD

OH, IT'S *OKAY*. I THINK OWEN GUMMED IT UP PRETTY BADLY *ANYWAY*.

BESS, EASY! IF YOU COVER IT COMPLETELY, *NO ONE* WILL FIND IT!

THERE. *THAT'S* BETTER.

AND DON'T WORRY!

I'LL HAVE IT RUNNING AS GOOD AS NEW AFTER WE CATCH THE THIEF!

IT WAS A SIMPLE PLAN. I FIGURED OWEN SAW THE CROOK, AND IF HE HEARD THE CAMCORDER WAS MISSING, *THIS* WOULD BE THE *FIRST* PLACE HE'D LOOK.

AFTER AN *HOUR*, BESS DECIDED TO REASSURE GEORGE WITH A *LONG* DESCRIPTION OF HOW SHE COULD FIX HER CAMCORDER.

THE PLASTIC THINGS WITH THE GREEN AND YELLOW CIRCUITS. EVEN IF ONE CRACKS, YOU JUST *REPLACE* IT!

BUT BESS IS AN *INTUITIVE* REPAIR-GAL, MEANING SHE DOESN'T ALWAYS KNOW WHAT TO CALL ALL THE PIECES.

THEN YOU JUST SNAP THE YELLOW WHATSIS INTO THE FLAT COPPER THING BEHIND THE LENS.

IT'LL BE FINE. TRUST ME.

JUST AS LONG AS IT DOESN'T GET *RAINED* ON OR ANYTHING.

KSSHHHHHHH!

HUSH! I HEAR SOMEONE *COMING!*

KEEP IT DOWN! HE'LL *HEAR* US!

WHICH, OF COURSE, HE *DID*.

FUNNY HOW THIS WHOLE CASE STARTED WITH A RAINSTORM AND AN ACCIDENT WITH AN SUV.

NOW IT LOOKED LIKE IT MIGHT *END* THAT WAY AS WELL!

KAVRMMMMM

WE LOST HIM!

NO! HE COULDN'T HAVE GOTTEN THAT FAR ON *FOOT*!

DO YOU GUYS HEAR SOMETHING WEIRD, LIKE A *LAWN-MOWER*?

OR AN SUV! RUN!

GRGGNNGNNG

HE'S GETTING AWAY! I'LL CALL MCGINNIS!

IF HE REACHES THE ROAD, WE'LL *NEVER* FIND HIM!

ANOTHER THING ABOUT SUVS IS THAT THEY HAVE A HIGHER CENTER OF *GRAVITY* AND RELATIVELY NARROWER WHEEL-TRACK THAN REGULAR PASSENGER CARS.

THIS MAKES THEM *PARTICULARLY* SUSCEPTIBLE TO ROLLOVERS.

IN FACT, STATISTICALLY, SUVS HAVE THE *HIGHEST* ROLLOVER INVOLVEMENT RATE OF *ANY* VEHICLE TYPE!

AND, IN 1999, ROLLOVERS WERE RESPONSIBLE FOR 63% OF THE FATALITIES IN SUV ACCIDENTS.

SO OUR DRIVER GOT VERY *LUCKY* HERE.

BUT NOW THAT WE WERE *ALL* ON FOOT, SLOGGING UPHILL THROUGH MUD AND RAIN, THE ODDS WERE MORE *EVEN*.

WHAT'S ON THE OTHER SIDE OF THIS HILL?

IF I REMEMBER, IT'S ABOUT A TWO HUNDRED FOOT *DROP* INTO THE RIVER!

I'VE HAD SOME CROOKS TELL ME ONE OF THE REASONS THEY *LIKED* TO COMMIT CRIMES WAS THE FEELING THEY GET WHEN THEY THINK THEY'VE GOTTEN AWAY WITH IT.

IT WAS THE ONLY TIME IN THEIR LIVES WHEN THEY FELT LIKE A LITTLE KID AGAIN.

LIKE OWEN, MAYBE, GETTING AWAY WITH STEALING SOME COOKIES FOR HIMSELF.

THE ONLY PROBLEM, FOR THE THIEF, IS THAT THE MOMENT NEVER REALLY *LASTS* VERY LONG.

81

AT LEAST NOT IF *I* HAVE ANYTHING TO SAY ABOUT IT.

THE TAPE DOESN'T MATTER. I HAVE ALL THE PROOF I NEED.

AND *I KNOW* WHO YOU ARE.

PRO- FESSOR SEVERE.

THEN I ASSUME YOU MADE *COPIES* OF THE TAPE, YES?

"THEN THERE WERE THE SAMPLES FROM WENTLEY'S BASEMENT. THEY *WERE* ANCIENT LIMESTONE, *NOT* CONCRETE LIKE YOU SAID.

"YOU'RE AN *EXPERT*, SO YOU *MUST* HAVE BEEN *LYING*."

"AND THERE'S *MORE*."

"OWEN SAID HE KICKED THE STRANGER IN THE LEG. I REMEMBERED YOU *LIMPING*.

"FOR SOME REASON, YOU'VE BEEN WORKING WITH WENTLEY!"

I JUST DON'T UNDER-STAND *WHY*! WHY HAVE YOUR OWN ARTIFACT *STOLEN* AND *DESTROYED*?

WELL, I DIDN'T HAVE IT *STOLEN*. THAT WAS MR. WENTLEY'S DOING. QUITE AN INTERESTING FELLOW, REALLY.

YOU *SAY* I'M AN EXPERT, BUT I MISSED SOMETHING VERY *OBVIOUS* ABOUT THE MARKER...

...SOMETHING *YOU* BROUGHT TO MY ATTENTION WHEN YOU WONDERED HOW *HARD* IT MUST HAVE BEEN TO RAISE A *CHILD* ON A SEA VOYAGE.

IT WAS LIKE A *LIGHT* GOING ON IN MY HEAD. ADMIRAL CHENG HO NEVER *HAD* ANY CHILDREN.

HE COULDN'T – HE WAS A *EUNUCH.* IT'S A MATTER OF RECORD.

EVERY CHILD IN CHINA WOULD HAVE KNOWN THE STONE WAS FAKE! I WOULD HAVE BECOME A *LAUGHING* STOCK!

RIGHTLY SO. I FELT LIKE SUCH A *FOOL.*

NUMBLY, I WENT ON WITH THE PRESENTATION. I STILL *BELIEVED* THE THEORY AFTER ALL.

THEN WENTLEY STOLE THE MARKER, AND CONTACTED ME FOR A *RANSOM*.

HE WAS A LITTLE *SURPRISED* WHEN INSTEAD I OFFERED TO PAY HIM TO *DESTROY* IT.

BUT MONEY WAS MONEY, AND HE'S *VERY* FOND OF MONEY.

WHEN I HEARD ABOUT THE *TAPE*, I WAS AFRAID WENTLEY WOULD BE CAUGHT AND HE'D, HOW DO THOSE GANGSTERS SAY IT, "RAT ME OUT"?

YOU KNOW THE REST.

BUT *TELL* ME, IS IT A *CRIME* TO DESTROY A *FAKE* ARTIFACT?

WELL, *NO*, IT'S NOT. BUT, AS CHIEF McGINNIS EXPLAINED, TRYING TO RUN PEOPLE DOWN WITH AN SUV *IS*. SO IS NOT REPORTING THE LOCATION OF A MISSING CHILD!

PROFESSOR SEVERE DIDN'T UNDERSTAND IT HAD *NOTHING* TO DO WITH THE ARTIFACT, JUST WITH THE FACT THAT HE NO LONGER CARED *WHO* HE HURT TO PROTECT HIMSELF.

STILL, AS A FIRST OFFENDER, *HE'D* GET A LIGHT SENTENCE.

NOT SO "POOR" MR. WENTLEY. BASED ON PROFESSOR SEVERE'S CONFESSION, THE POLICE WERE ABLE TO SUBPOENA ALL *FIFTEEN* OF HIS BANK ACCOUNTS.

TURNS OUT HE'D BEEN STEALING FROM THE MUSEUM, *AND* HIS OTHER TWO JOBS FOR *YEARS!* ALL TOLD, HE'D SAVED A QUARTER MILLION IN STOLEN LOOT!

LIKE I SAID, THERE ARE AS MANY DIFFERENT KINDS OF CROOKS AS THERE ARE *PEOPLE*.